the CLeo STORieS

A Friend
and
A Pet

For my storytelling mum,
Gwynne ~ L.G.

For cool Uncle Sendo ~ F.B.

the CLeO STORieS

A Friend *and* A Pet

Libby Gleeson ★ Freya Blackwood

ALLEN & UNWIN
SYDNEY · MELBOURNE · AUCKLAND · LONDON

Cleo

makes a friend

Cleo McCann is staring at the rain.

Drip, drip, drip.
A puddle is forming
on the back step.

'Cleo,' calls Mum, 'I want you to tidy your room.'

'I can't.'

'Why? What are you doing?'

'Counting raindrops.'

'How many are you up to?'

'Lots and lots.'

'Well, come and give me a hand,' Mum says. 'I'm making a pot of soup for lunch. You can shell the peas.'

Cleo shakes her head. 'I'm counting till I get up to a zillion.' She presses her nose hard against the window.

At lunch Cleo slurps small spoonfuls of vegetable soup.

'I hear you've been counting raindrops,' says Dad.

Cleo nods.

'How many did you get up to?'

'Sixty hundred.'

'Wow.'

'After lunch I'm going to count to a zillion.'
She looks through the window over the sink.
The rain has almost stopped.

'No more counting,' says Mum.
'Why don't we call Nick's family?
He could come over and play.'

'He's gone away,' says Cleo,
'to his uncle's farm. He's
going to feed the lambs
and the calves and see
the new puppies that
got born last week.'

'Well,' says Mum, 'then we'll just tidy your room. You've got toys and clothes all over the floor.'

'That's no fun, Mum.'

'And when you've cleaned your room, then you can play with your toys or read a book or ...'

'Double no fun.'

Mum takes the bowls to the sink. She comes back to wipe down the table. 'What's this?' She stares at a splodge of green dripping over the edge and onto the floor.

'It's celery. You know I hate it.' Cleo stares at her lap.

6

'You don't squash food and take it out of your bowl.
If you don't like it, just leave it. You're not a baby.'

Cleo goes and flops on the lounge-room floor.
She picks at the tiny hole in the carpet. A purple
thread is loose and she pulls it and winds it around
her finger.

'Cleo,' says Mum, 'you know not to do that.
You'll just make that hole bigger.'

Cleo tries to push the thread back into
the weave. It doesn't go.
She tucks it under
the carpet.

'Why don't you call another friend? Nick isn't your only one. What about Mia or Sophie?'

Cleo lifts herself up and rests her head on the coffee table. 'They had a sleepover last night. Just them and no one else. They're probably staying all weekend.'

'Okay, what about Isabella?'

'I don't like her anymore.'

'Why? What happened?'

'She told everyone Nick was my boyfriend and they all laughed.'

'That's silly. He's a good friend. That's all.'

'I know. Anyway I don't like her.'

'Well, don't just mope around here. I don't know what's got into you today. Off you go, up to your bedroom and tidy the things on the floor.'

Cleo drags herself to her feet and heads up the hallway. She scrapes her hand along under the pictures. She stops at Mum and Dad's room. The door is open. Cleo can see Mum's make-up spread across the dressing table. She goes in and shuts the door quietly.

Cleo sits on the stool and stares at herself in the
mirror. She pushes aside jars of face cream and flat
containers of coloured eye shadow. She picks up
a gold tube of lipstick. She pulls the top off and
sees the bright-red tube inside.

Cleo swipes it across her lips. It's hard to keep
to the line and when her hand shakes she puts
a splodge on her chin. She picks up some mascara.
She's watched Mum use the thin stick to dust
black over her eyelashes.

Cleo opens her left eye as wide as she can and dabs at the lashes. She misses. The stick goes into her eye. She blinks, screws her face up and lets out a cry. The mascara slides through her hand to the floor. Black dye covers her fingers, and slashes of it are now on the carpet.

Mum is in the doorway. 'Cleopatra Miranda McCann, what do you think you are doing?'

Tears run over Cleo's cheeks.

'You know not to play in here. I've told you that before. Go down to the laundry where there is some strong soap and wash your hands.'

Cleo walks slowly back along the hall and into the kitchen.

Uncle Tom is making himself a coffee. 'What's up, pumpkin? You've got a face as long as a wet week.'

Cleo shrugs. 'There's no one to play with and nothing to do.'

'You've got an imagination,' says Uncle Tom. 'Use it. Make something up.'

Cleo frowns. She goes through to the laundry and scrubs and scrubs at her hands. Then she goes outside.

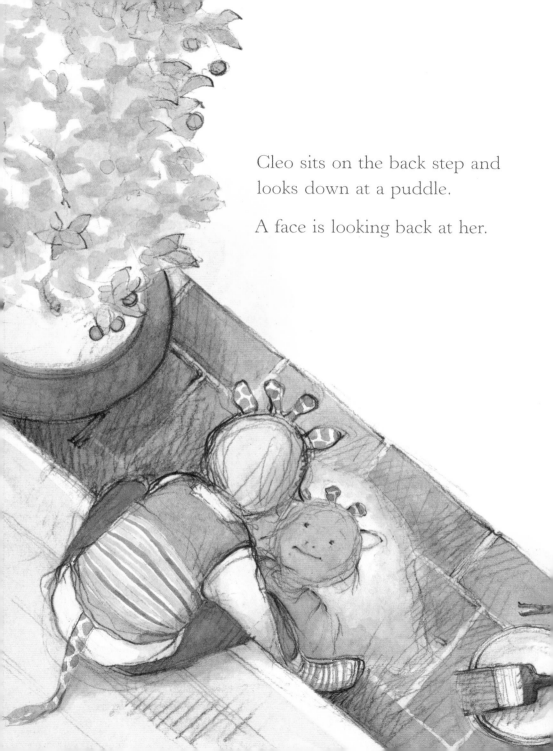

Cleo sits on the back step and looks down at a puddle.

A face is looking back at her.

Cleo closes one eye.

The face closes one eye.

Cleo sticks her finger in her mouth.

The face sticks a finger in its mouth.

Cleo takes a stick and stirs the water in the puddle.
The face wobbles but doesn't disappear.

Cleo starts to grin.

The face grins.

Cleo folds her arms and stares.
The face stares back at her.

Cleo giggles. She suddenly has an idea.

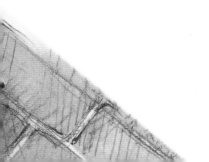

She almost runs back into the house.
Up the hallway she goes, leaping from
one square in the carpet to the next,
straight to her own room. She closes
the door and turns to face the mess.

A few minutes later Mum knocks on Cleo's door.
'Can I come in?'

'No.'

'What are you doing?'

'Nothing.'

'I hope you're cleaning up your room.'

'We are, kind of.'

'We?'

'I mean me.'

'Well, come and tell me when you are finished. I want to check on it and see that everything's been put away.'

Cleo doesn't answer.

After a while Dad comes up the hallway.
He is singing a crazy song.

'*A wonderful star is Cleo McCann,*
and I'm her dad, her greatest fan.'

He knocks on the door.

Cleo doesn't answer.

'Cleo?'

'I'm busy.'

'Can I come in?'

'No.'

'What are you doing?'

'None of your beeswax, Dad.'

'I beg your pardon.'

'Sorry, Dad.' Cleo is laughing. 'I'll let you know
when I'm finished.'

After about half an hour Cleo goes to the kitchen.
'You can come and look now.' She beckons her
parents.

Outside her room she puts up her hand to stop
them. 'You have to shut your eyes.' She takes them
by the hands and leads them through her door.

'Da daaa.' Cleo throws her arm towards
the centre of the room.

'My magic city,' she says. She points
to the teddy. 'And she's the boss,
checking up on everything.'

'You've never made anything like this before,' says Mum.

'My friend showed me.'

'Your friend?'

'Casey.'

'Who?'

'Casey Pickles. She comes from a city like this.'

Mum frowns. 'Where is this Casey? I'd like to meet her.'

Cleo hesitates. She glances around the room. 'She had to go.'

'You mean out the window?' says Mum.

'No. Don't be silly. She… she's in behind there.' Cleo points to the mirror. 'She's not coming out. She only likes talking to me. She's shy.'

Cleo hesitates again. 'She says I'm her very best friend in the whole wide world.'

Cleo

wants a pet

Cleo is watching Dad water the garden.

'Did you have a pet when you were
little like me?' she says.

'No,' says Dad. 'Aunty Amy had a big fish tank with lots of fish in it. I used to sit and watch them sometimes. Why do you ask?'

'Nick's got a new puppy and he's calling it Peanut. Can I get a puppy too? Then my puppy and Nick's puppy could play together.'

'I don't think so,' Dad says. 'Dogs take lots of work. You have to look after them and feed them every day.'

'I could do that.'

'And you have to give them a bath.'

'Nick says you can do that with the hose.'

'And take them for walks.'

'That's easy. Nick says he takes Peanut for a walk in the park every afternoon. I could go with them.'

'And dogs aren't cheap. It costs money to buy a dog.'

'You could take all my pocket money for the rest of the year.'

'I don't think so.'

'You could take my pocket money till … till I go to the big school past the shops.'

'That's high school, Cleo. That's years away.'

'But I truly, ruly want a puppy.'

'Puppies love to dig up the garden and we've just made this vegie patch. You wouldn't want it wrecked, would you?'

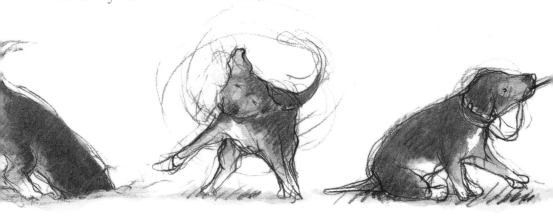

The next afternoon, Cleo goes to Nick's place after
school. Peanut is in a box on the back verandah.

'Peanut,' calls Nick. 'Peanut.'

The puppy jumps out of the box into Nick's arms.
Nick falls down flat on his bottom and Peanut's pink
tongue slobbers all over his face.

Cleo cannot take her eyes away.

After a few minutes, Nick picks up Peanut and puts her in Cleo's lap.

'Look,' he says, feeling around Peanut's neck for her collar. There on a flat metal disc is the word 'Peanut' and Nick's phone number.

Cleo pats the puppy's head. Peanut nuzzles under her arm.

Cleo puts both arms around her and gives her the biggest hug. Peanut licks Cleo's neck and pees all over Cleo's school dress.

Nick laughs.

Cleo pushes Peanut away. Her dress is damp and smelly but she laughs too.

35

Later, in the car, Mum sniffs. 'You smell like dog,' she says.

'Mum,' says Cleo, 'Nick says his dog comes from his uncle who lives on a farm. It didn't cost them any money.'

'That's good for Nick,' says Mum, 'but we don't
have an uncle who lives on a farm.'

'Why can't Uncle Tom live on a farm?'

'Because your Uncle Tom works in the city,
like Dad and I do,' says Mum.

When they get home Cleo finds Uncle Tom.
'I wish you lived on a farm,' she says.

'Why's that, pumpkin?'

'Because then you'd have dogs
and you could give one to me.'

'You could get another pet. When I was a little bloke,
I had a blue-tongue lizard, and I had a mate who
kept rats in a cage in his bedroom.'

'I don't think Mum and Dad would like that,'
says Cleo.

It's Friday night pizza dinner.

'It's not fair,' says Cleo.

'I thought you liked pizza,' says Dad as he takes
a big slice.

'I'm not talking about that.' Cleo picks an olive
off her piece and puts it in her mouth. 'At school
today Mr French made us talk about our pets.
And everyone has a pet but me.'

'Everyone?' says Mum.

'Everyone,' says Cleo. 'Well, everyone but Stella and Jessie and Alfie and me.'

'Has anyone got rats or lizards?' says Uncle Tom.

Cleo shakes her head. 'Tom's got chooks and Isabella's got a bunny rabbit called Blossom and Sophie's got a cat called Tinkerbelle and it might have kittens and if it does she says I can have one. Can I, Mum? Can I?'

'I don't know,' says Mum. 'Cats are a worry. You have to keep them in at night because they chase the birds and the skinks in the garden and if you go away you have to find someone to feed them. It's like that with all pets.'

'Nick would do that for me,' says Cleo.

On Saturday afternoon,
it's Cleo's job to help Dad in the garden.
They are weeding the tomatoes and beans and
parsley and basil. Some of the leaves have
big holes nibbled in them. Some leaves
have been completely chewed away.

'It's those snails,' says Dad.
He sprinkles small green pellets
between the rows of plants.

'What does that do?'

'Kills them. Snails eat the
pellets and it kills them.'

'That's cruel, Dad. You're a murderer.'

'It's them or us,' says Dad. 'You like eating our fresh vegies from the garden don't you?'

Cleo nods.

'Then we have to get rid of the pests.'

'But they're little,' says Cleo. 'They can't help it.'

'Maybe, but they eat their way through all the things we like to eat too.'

'Well, I don't want to eat these vegies anymore.'

'I thought you liked them.'

Cleo shakes her head. 'Not now. I hate them.'

'Cleopatra Miranda McCann, you will eat your
vegies. If you don't want to help me grow them,
go off to your room and play at something else.'

'I will,' says Cleo and she
stomps into the house.

Cleo sits at the kitchen table. She has Mum's big scissors and she's cutting up old magazines, searching for pictures of pets.

She finds fluffy white cats, and kittens with sleek black fur and blue eyes. There are dogs of all shapes and sizes. One is almost as tall as a pony and others look like rats.

In a story about the Easter Show, Cleo finds golden guinea pigs, two champion white rabbits and a family with ducks. Some schoolchildren have their own chicken coop with three hens and lots of tiny golden chickens inside.

Cleo tries to imagine which pet she would like.
Which pet would feel right in her backyard?
A rabbit? A rooster? A guinea pig? Which pet
would Mum and Dad let her have? Will they
always say no?

Cleo looks out into the garden. Dad has the big
gardening fork and is digging up a new section
of the vegie patch. Cleo stares and stares.

Then she has an idea.
A special, secret idea.

Cleo goes to her room and
changes into her cat-burglar
clothes. She takes the shoebox
from her new school shoes and
tiptoes down the hall.

Dad and Uncle Tom have gone
into the shed. The phone rings
and Cleo hears Mum going
into the kitchen to answer it.
Mum is laughing and saying
something to Aunty Amy.
Good. That will take a while.

Cleo ducks quickly outside.

After dinner, when Cleo is tucked up in bed, Mum reads her a story. It's all about a dog called Harry who loves having adventures and getting dirty. It's Cleo's favourite. She wonders if Peanut would like to roll in the dirt like Harry.

Dad comes in and sits on the end of Cleo's bed. 'Mum and I have been thinking,' he says. 'We know you really want to get a pet and maybe we've been too quick to say no. You're big enough to look after something. So...'

Cleo grins. 'It's okay. I don't need a pet now. I've got five.'

'Five?' says Dad.

'Five?' says Mum.

'Five,' says Cleo, smiling. She throws back the blanket and climbs out of bed. She takes the shoebox from her wardrobe and hands it to them.

Inside, shiny green leaves and grass line the bottom. Slowly sliding under and over them, leaving their silver trails behind, are five big, fat snails.

'Five,' grins Cleo again.

Libby Gleeson lives in Sydney in a big house that used
to have her, her husband, her three daughters, a cat,
two guinea pigs, three rabbits, a budgie and lots and lots
of pet mice. The daughters have grown up and left home,
the budgie flew away and all the others are now buried
under the vegie patch. Her husband is still fine.

Freya Blackwood lives in Orange, New South Wales,
with her daughter and *lots* of pets. The pets need feeding every
day, dig up the garden and poo everywhere — but Freya and her
daughter *love* them! They have a dog called Pivot, five chickens
and a rabbit called Quartz. They are
also looking after a duck with a sore leg.

LiBBY

by Cleo

FrEYa
by cleo

First published by Allen & Unwin in 2015

Allen & Unwin – Australia
83 Alexander Street, Crows Nest NSW 2065, Australia
Phone: (61 2) 8425 0100
Email: info@allenandunwin.com
Web: www.allenandunwin.com

Allen & Unwin – UK
c/o Murdoch Books, Erico House, 93-99 Upper Richmond Road, London SW15 2TG, UK
Phone: (44 20) 8785 5995
Email: info@murdochbooks.co.uk
Web: www.allenandunwin.com
Murdoch Books is a wholly owned division of Allen & Unwin Pty Ltd

A Cataloguing-in-Publication entry is available
from the National Library of Australia
www.trove.nla.gov.au.
A catalogue record for this book is available from the British Library

ISBN (AUS) 978 1 74331 528 6
ISBN (UK) 978 1 74336 706 3

Cover and text design by Sandra Nobes
Set in 14.5 pt Horley Old Style by Sandra Nobes
Colour reproduction by Splitting Image, Clayton, Victoria
This book was printed in May 2016 at Hang Tai Printing (Guang Dong) Ltd., China.

www.libbygleeson.com.au
www.freyablackwood.net

3 5 7 9 10 8 6 4